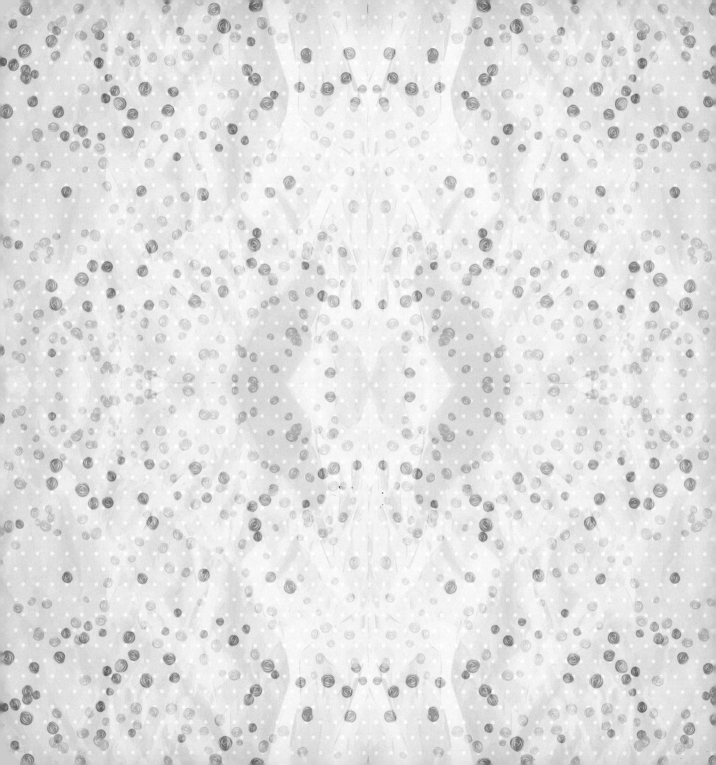

TIME TOGETHER

Me and Dad

BY MARIA CATHERINE

ILLUSTRATED BY PASCAL CAMPION

PICTURE WINDOW BOOKS

THIS BOOK BELONGS TO:

- -

Favorite song time

Colorful family portrait time

Fancy tea party time

Fairy tale time

Cookie baking time

Bear hug time

Quiet talking time

Sky-high building time

Wild ride time

Dog walking time

Falling leaves time

Shiny smile time

Sweet dream time

Time Together is published by Picture Window Books
A Capstone Imprint
1710 Roe Crest Drive
North Mankato, Minnesota 56003
www.capstonepub.com

Library of Congress Cataloging-in-Publication data
is available on the Library of Congress website.
ISBN: 978-1-4795-2253-8 (paper over board)
ISBN: 978-1-4795-2255-2 (paperback)

Summary:
Snapshots of a dad and child enjoying
every day moments together.

Concepted by:
Kay Fraser and Christianne Jones

Designer:
K. Fraser

Photo Credit:
Shutterstock

Printed in China by Nordica.
1013/CA21301928
092013   007751NORDS14

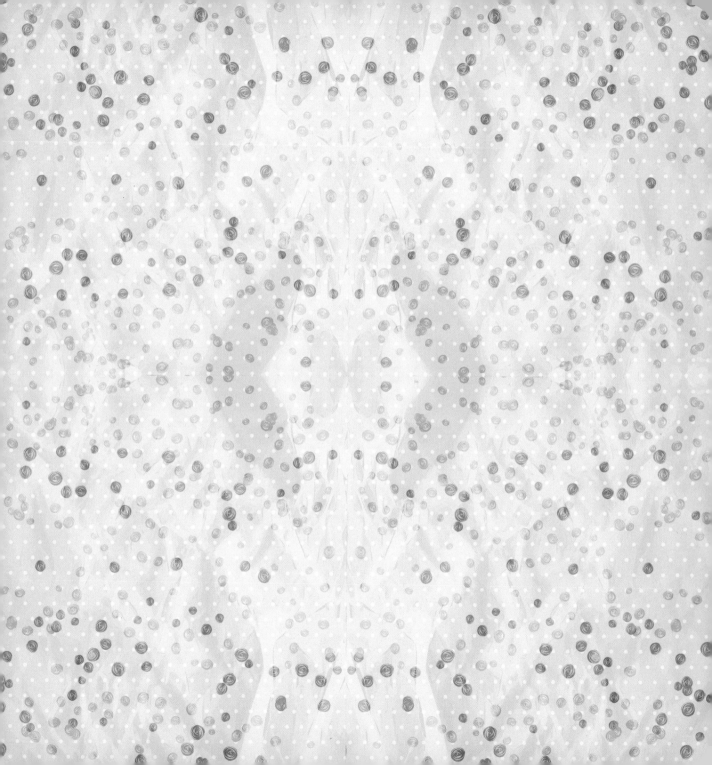